The House of
Chelten Ham

DAVID EDSALL

ISBN   978-1-64552-190-7   (Paperback)
ISBN   978-1-64552-189-1   (Digital)

Lettra Press books may be ordered through booksellers or by contacting:

Lettra Press LLC
30 N Gould St. Suite 4753
Sheridan, WY 82801
1 307-200-3414 | info@lettrapress.com
www.lettrapress.com

Contents

Chapter One

Breaking The Writer's Block

It's Monday morning and Pam diverts her attention from a TV talk show to glance toward the closed door of one of the two bedrooms that are part of their New York Bronx apartment. Her husband, Mike, has turned it into his own personal man cave. Her thoughts are interrupted by the sound of their doorbell. "Who could be so rude to bother me, unannounced in the middle of my talk show," Pam thinks to herself as she slowly rises from her couch and heads for the front door.

When she opens the door and sees the person standing there, she is mixed with emotions. Trying on a forced smile, "Lonnie! Hello. What brings you here on this Friday morning?" she asks as if she didn't know.

"Hello, Pam. How's my favorite lady? Just thought I'd drop by and see how Mike is coming along with our next novel."

"Yes, I was wondering that myself," Pam thought quietly to herself. "Well, come in. He's in his cave. You know where it is."

Lonnie knocks on the bedroom/cave door and then opens it without waiting for an invitation. Mike looks up from his desk. "Oh, hi Lonnie," Mike says without expressing any notion that he is glad to see him.

"How are we coming with our next book?" Lonnie asked as he looks around. "We're coming," Mike answers. Lonnie checks out the top of Mikes desk for any sign of finished pages. The desk is loaded with wadded up sheets of typing paper. Lonnie notices the same wads of paper filling the trash can by Mike's desk as well as a fair amount spilling out onto the floor.

Mike leans back, looking defeated. "Have you got something for me to read?" Lonnie presses. After a short pause Mike answers, "The New York Times is laying over there."

Lonnie lowers himself into the chair that is sitting near Mikes desk. "Hey man, you got to give me something. Something soon." "I know. I'm just having trouble finding a start." Well, you better start something soon. The publisher will be wanting back that fat advance you got. "I know. Just get out of here and let me get to it.

Lonnie rises from the chair. "OK, buddy. Call me next week. Better still, email me a few pages so I have something to show. By the way, if you would give up that old typewriter and use a computer, you could save a lot of trees." Lonnie turns, with a smile, and leaves Mike to continue writing. As he passes thru the living room Pam looks up from the TV. "How's he coming?" she asked. Lonnie shakes his head. "He's got a really bad case of writers' block. You need to get him motivated, somehow." Lonnie departs the front door without waiting for a comment from Pam.

Mike quietly walks into the living room and sits down on an easy chair near the couch that Pam is sitting on. They look at each other without a word. Pam reaches over for the TV remote and lowers the volume. She remains quiet.

"I don't know what I'm going to do. Ever since we moved to the Bronx and into this apartment, I can't seem to get my creative juices flowing." "You think it's because of this apartment," Pam asked. Mike purches his lips and looks down at the floor in deep thought. "I don't think it's just this apartment," he finally says. Pam is quietly waiting on him to continue. "I think our whole life style, here in the city, is wrong for me." "I seem to recall you wanted to move here to be closer to your agency," Pam answered. "I know."

"I don't understand what difference it makes if you are writing in a closed room in this apartment or some closed room out in the sticks of America," Pam commented.

At first Mike didn't answer. He just stared into space trying to analyze Pam's words. After more than a minute, "I once read in the biography of Somerset Mom, that he only wrote four hours per day. After that he found other things to do. If you think about it, I always had other interest, other projects, to work on when I wasn't writing. I have no interests here except writing. Nothing to look forward to, to fill up the rest of my day, when I am finished writing."

Pam listened intently but remained quiet. Mike looked at her, then back down at the floor. After what seem an eternity, Pam broke the silence. "So, what's the answer?"

Mike continued looking at the floor then slowly raised his head and peered into Pam's eyes. "I want to leave here." "Ok. We don't have a lease so we can leave anytime. Do you want me to start looking for a different apartment?"

Mike pinched his lips together, then, shook his head no. "I want to leave New York altogether; a complete change of atmosphere." Pam stares at him a few moments before she asks, "Where do you want to go, Philly?" "No. Midwest." Mike raises his head and looks at Pam for several seconds before speaking. "I have found a mini farm with an old farmhouse in the middle of Indiana. That's where I want to be. That's where I think I can write. That's where I can feed chickens and pick corn from our garden." Mike stops short, waiting for Pam to explode.

Pam stares at Mike with her mouth open. Mike thinks, "She is in shock." Mike breaks the silence. "The old farmhouse is over one-hundred years old. It does need work, but that, too, is something we can do together." Pam slowly closes her mouth. She draws a deep breath. "I think I saw this movie. Wasn't it called 'The Money Pit'?

Chapter Two

The Old Cheltenham House

Mike and Pam are winding their way along the crooked backland roads of east central Indiana in their newly acquired used Jeep. They are headed for the small village of Brownsville, the closest grocery store, about 2 miles from their house.

"Darling, I'm glad you decided to come with me to the grocery. You've been working so hard on that old house." "Oh, now it's an old house," Mike replied. "You know what I mean. Besides, it is an old house. After all it is over one-hundred years old. But it's a wonderful old house. I can't wait until we get it finished."

Mike smiles. "I know, we'll get it done one of these days. It's just that it takes so long to do everything, not to mention the four hours I spend writing each day." "Well, at least you are writing at long last. The house is coming along ok, and there really isn't any hurry. Except, I mean, to finish your novel. We are going to need the money. Otherwise, you could hire some help. Mike nodded in agreement. "Actually," Pam added, "I'm not sure you can find anyone to go out there anyway."

"Why?" Mike questioned. "You haven't been going with me to Brownsville for groceries that often. You've been buying all your materials and supplies in Connersville. I get the sense that locally, people pretty much try to avoid the old Cheltenham house." Mike nods again. "I've heard some of those wild tales about Dr. Cheltenham, but he's been dead for almost forty years. Besides, those rumors are the reason we got the place so cheap." "I know. But, I don't want to talk about old man Cheltenham. I'd rather think about when we finish the house and can give some serious thought to starting a family," Pam said with a grin. Mike glanced at her with a wryer smile.

The Jeep rounds their last turn and enters the town. Mike pulls up in front of the only grocery. As they step from the Jeep Mike says, "You go on and start gathering the groceries. I want to see if I can find an electrician willing to come out to the house. I can't figure what is wrong with the basement lights." Pam nods and heads for the front door of the grocery.

The grocer looks up from behind the counter. He recognizes Pam and smiles. "I see the goblins haven't chased you guys away from the Cheltenham house yet," he comments with a grin. Pam nods and smiles as she heads for the first grocery item on her list. "We aren't afraid of no stinkin ghosts. Besides, we're meaner than they are anyway."

Pam is busy gathering up her groceries. She didn't notice the automobile that pulled up in front. Nor, did she pay any attention to the man entering the store. Stopping at the check-out counter he asks, "Excuse me. I'm wondering if you can help me. I'm looking for an old house that shouldn't be too far from here. I thought you may have heard of it. It was recently purchased by a couple from New York." The clerk looks surprised as he glances toward Pam. "Do you mean the old Cheltenham house?" he asks.

The clerk looks back at Pam as she whirls around at the mention of her house. With surprise on her face she exclaims, "Lonnie? Lonnie Harris? Is that you?" Lonnie turns quickly in the direction of Pam's voice. "Pam? He questions loudly. He moves toward her. "What luck, finding you here just as I arrive." "Yes," Pam answers. "But, what in the world are you doing here?" Pam moves to the check-out counter and puts down her groceries. The clerk begins adding up her items. "Oh, I decided to get away from the city for a while. I wanted to see what you and Mike find so appealing out here in these hills." "Uhh, Hhh. You just want to see if Mike is actually working on the novel." Lonnie grins. "Is he?" "Well, you'll just have to wait and see." "Is Mike back at the house?" "No, he's around here somewhere looking for an electrician." "You mean you actually have electricity?" "Yes," Pam smiles. "Everywhere except the basement. You know you came at the worst possible time. We are in the process of tearing up and fixing just about everything." "That's ok. Maybe I can help. I can find a motel." "The nearest one would be in Connersville, about 10 miles away. But, I'm sure we can find you a bed and a bedroom. The two bedrooms were the first rooms we finished after we completed updating the kitchen."

Pam pays the grocer and heads outside for the Jeep. Lonnie grabs some of the sacks and follows her out. They deposit the groceries into the Jeep and Lonnie asks, "What now?" "I'm supposed to meet Mike here." Pam looks up and down the street then across the street. "Here he comes," she exclaims.

Mike crosses the street and a smile breaks out on his face as he recognizes Lonnie, His literary agent. "Look whose here," Pam says as Mike approaches. "Well, well. I thought I left you in New York." "I was beginning to wish I was in New York, after driving these crooked gravel roads." "You haven't seen anything yet. Wait til you see the road leading to our house, not to mention our long driveway. That's why I bought this Jeep."

"Pam tells me you are having electrical problems." "Yes, and I can't find anyone, let alone an electrician, that will go near the place." What have you got out there?. Maybe I don't want to go," Lonnie says with a grin. "Well, we have flies, mosquitos, ticks and fresh air." Lonnie sighs. "Well, I'm not sure I can handle the fresh air, but let's give it a try. You know, it just so happens that I'm somewhat of an electrician. I worked my way through college as an electrician's helper." "Really?" Pam chimed in. "Great," Mike says. Let's get going then."

Lonnie falls in behind Mike and Pam's Jeep and they wind their way towards the Cheltenham House. Mike slows and then turns into a narrow and rutty lane that proceeds up the side of a hill. No house was in sight at the lane's entrance. As Lonnie turned in behind the Jeep, he glanced at the power lines leading from the utility pole and heading up the hill. The number of power lines seemed strange, but he didn't have time to belabor the thought. Missing potholes and ruts in the lane demanded all of his attention. "I'm glad I rented this Jeep."

As they rounded a curve at the top of the hill Lonnie got his first look at the house. It's total two-story stone structure, sitting high on this hill gave it an eary look. "No wonder people don't want to come out here," Lonnie thought to himself. He pulled in behind Mike's Jeep and pushed the button to open the trunk. "Can I help?" Mike asks as he climbs out of the Jeep. "No, I travel light." Lonnie pulls out two medium size suitcases and shuts the trunk. Standing, with a suitcase in each hand he takes another look at the old house. With a sigh and raised eyebrows he follows Pam and Mike. They enter the front door and Mike says, "Well, this is it. Let me put down the groceries and I'll show you around."

The entrance way was spacious. To the right was the kitchen/dining room and to the left was the living room. Straight ahead was a staircase leading to the second floor. Lonnie put down his bags at the bottom of the stairway and followed Pam into the living room. "Mike finished the kitchen first so we could prepare meals on something better than a camp stove. Then he finished the upstairs two bedrooms which were the easiest to finish. The living room is next along with the basement," Pam reported.

"So, where does he spend his time writing?" Lonnie asked. Pam looked at him and made a frown. "Now don't you start on him. He's working four hours every day on it. He uses the second bedroom, upstairs, as a combination bedroom and study." "The bedroom I will occupy?" Lonnie asked. "Yes." "Well, then I will set my alarm early in the morning so as not to get in the way of his work," Lonnie said with a grin.

Mike enters the living room. "Why don't you show Lonnie around. I've got to start dinner," Pam said. "Ok, we can start upstairs. I can show you your room first."

Lonnie leans back from the dinner table. "I feel like a new man." "Yes, I thought dinner was extra good tonight dear," Mike said to Pam. "Mike, let's have a look at the basement." "Now?" Mike asks. "Sure. Never put off til tomorrow what you can do today." "Ok. I'll get a couple flashlights."

Mike leads the way down the basement stairway. Overhead is a sloping ceiling that is the bottom of the upper staircase. "Where is the fuse box for the house?" Lonnie asks. "It's just ahead on the wall at the end of these stairs." Lonnie walks up to the fuse box. He notices a three-inch pipe that houses the wires leading to the box. "Where is the meter?" Lonnie questioned. "It is outside on the other side of this wall. That is the front of the house."

Lonnie open the fuse box and observes three wires entering the box from inside the pipe. Everything seemed normal until Lonnie noticed the fuse labeled 'basement' did not have any wire coming from it. "Here is a problem," Lonnie said. "There is no basement circuit present in this box. Is there another fuse box?" "Not that I am aware of," Mike answers. Lonnie stares at the fuse box silently. He shakes his head in confusion. "What?" Mike finally asks. Lonnie looks at Mike. He shakes his head in an 'I don't know' fashion. He bites the edge of his lip. "It's something I saw when we first arrived. I didn't think so much of it at the time but," Lonnie stops mid-sentence and bites his lip again. Mike waits patiently for Lonnie to continue. Lonnie takes a deep breath then, "See here at the top of the fuse box. You have three wires coming in. Those wires are coming from the main utility pole out at the street where your lane begins. They pass through the meter outside and then through this pipe and into the box here." So?" "When we arrived this afternoon and entered your lane, I noticed six wires coming from the utility companies transformer and heading up your lane." "Where are the other three wires?" Mike asked. "That is the question. And, why. What for. You could run a small factory with that much power." Lonnie shuts the fuse box. "Tomorrow, in the daylight we'll try to solve this mystery." "Ok. Let's go have a night cap and then we can turn in," Mike offered. Lonnie smiled in agreement.

"Now, that's what I call breakfast," Lonnie exclaims as he pushes back from the table. "Thank you," Pam replied. Lonnie picks up his coffee cup takes the last sip. "Well, Mr, Martin. Shell we attack your electrical problem?" "Yes," Mike answered. "I want to go back to the head of your lane to start. Let's jump into your jeep," Lonnie suggested. The two headed down the lane to the electric companies' utility pole. "See, there are six wires coming from the transformer." "Transformer?" Mike questioned. "That tall round black thing." "Oh." "See, the six wires coming from it are leading over to your first private utility pole. Let's follow them in your jeep."

As Mike drives back up the driveway, Lonnie continues to follow the wires from pole to pole. When they come to the last pole, near the house, Lonnie yells, "Stop." He gets out of the Jeep and walks toward the utility pole. Mike follows. "Look here. Three of the lines continue over to your house and the electric meter. But, three are entering a 2 inch pipe that is running down the side of this pole." Mike looks up. "Do you see that?" Lonnie asks. "Yes.

Lonnie's eyes follows the pipe down the length of the utility pole. "It goes underground here. Where it goes from there, I'm not sure. But, I'd bet it is going to your house."

Lonnie walks toward the house as Mike returns to the Jeep and pulls it up to its' usual parking place. Lonnie is inspecting every inch of the exterior of the house. After making it around and back to the front he exclaims, "There is no evidence of those wires surfacing and no electric meter here on the outside. Let's go to the basement. Lonnie heads for the front door at a quick gait with Mike close behind. After grabbing a couple flashlights they descend the basement steps. Lonnie begins to inspect every inch of the outer walls of the basement which is also the foundation for the house. As he works his way to the front wall he sees what is a ledge protruding out from the top of the foundation.

"Is there something I can stand on. I want to see what is on top of that ledge between the floor joists." Mike looks around and see a stool sitting beside an old desk. "Will that stool work?" Lonnie looks in the direction of Mikes flashlight beam. "Yes, that will do nicely."

Lonnie places the stool at the corner of the basement where the ledge begins. Climbing onto the stool he inspects the spaces he can reach from the stool. Climbing down and moving the stool a little farther along the wall, he once again climbs up to look. "Wala," Lonnie shouts. "Another fuse box hidden up here." Lonnie opens the box and pears in. The three illusive wires present themselves as they come thru the foundation and into the electric box. Lonnie looks down at mike. "Those wires come out here and into this fuse box. The box is switched to off. I think somebody hid this box on purpose. I'm not sure what will happen if I flip it on." "Flip it on and see," Mike offered. Lonnie perched his mouth with a "Ummm."

Slowly he turned from Mike and reached for the lever on the side of the box. "Here goes nothing." Lonnie pushes the lever to the on position and suddenly the basement is bathed in light. "Wow, there be light," Mike exclaims. Lonnie smiles are he climbs from the stool. They look around the basement taking it all in for the first time. In the corner sat a desk. A small bookshelf rack just behind. "That must be where the good doctor did his work," Mike offered. Lonnie nodded.

"Well, that solves that problem," Mike says. "Well, yes and no." Mike looks quizzically at Lonnie. The power coming through that box up there is not coming thru a meter. This electricity is being stolen from the utility company." "How's that possible?" Mike asks. "Someone, for some reason, didn't want anyone to know about the consumption of your basements power. The power lines would have had to be strung in the dead of night." "Just for a few measly basement lights?" Lonnie shrugs his shoulders without answering. He walks over to the desk. The top is clear except for a desk light and an ink blotter. Pulling open the center drawer Lonnie sees a rather thick folder. He pulls it out and opens its' pages. "This appears to be his journal." Mike glances at Lonnie. Lonnie looks up from the journal. "I'll take it upstairs and read it tonight. Who knows, maybe I'll publish it.

That evening Lonnie settles onto his bed and opens Dr. Cheltenham's journal and begins to read.

"October 20, 1980. Dr. Harold Jacobs arrived this evening. We talked of old times. Tomorrow, I will show him the lab and explain the process to him. My hopes are that he will agree to work with me on the project. He must. I can't take no for an answer. Time is running out for me.

Chapter Three

Forty Years Earlier

Dr. Cheltenham is fidgeting around in the kitchen nervously waiting for a knock on the door. He looks at his watch. He pours himself a glass of wine and moves to the living room. Placing the wine on a table beside his favorite chair he prepares to sit down. A knock on the front door and he whirls around. "Finally." Upon opening the door, he sees his friend and colleague, Dr. Harold Jacobs. "Harold, so good to see you." They shake hands. "So good to have actually been able to find your house," Dr. Jacobs says with a smile. "Come in."

Dr. Cheltenham leads him into the entrance way. "Just put your bags down there Herold, I'll show you your room later. Can I get you something to drink? A glass of wine perhaps?" "Wine would be nice." "Ok. Go into the living room and find yourself a comfortable chair. I'll be in, in a second."

As the doctors socialize in the living room with mostly small talk Dr. Jacobs finally asks, "Hans, what are you doing here? Or, more to the point, what am I doing here?" "I have much to tell and indeed show you. But, we should wait until tomorrow. I assure you that you will find that your trip here was more than worthwhile. With that said, let me show you your room. You must be tired after your long trip from Philadelphia.. We'll get into everything tomorrow morning.

Dr. Jacob's eyes slowly opened. For a second, he wasn't sure where he was at. A glance at the clock showed 7:10 am. "Whoa. I've overslept. I must have been tired," he thought. The smell of breakfast entered his nose from the kitchen downstairs. After a quick shower he joined Dr. Cheltenham for breakfast.

"Ok, Hans. The suspense is killing me. I'm dying to find out why you sent for me," Dr. Jacobs remarked as he pushed his breakfast plate aside and finished the last of his coffee.

"Yes. Ok. I'll leave the dishes for later. Let me prepare you for what you are about to see and hear." In anticipation of, perhaps a lengthy introduction, he reaches over for the coffee pot and fills both their cups.

Dr. Cheltenham takes a deep breath, then begins. "Herold, do you know the date you are going to die?" Dr. Jacobs was about to take a sip of his coffee. Looking at Dr. Cheltenham he sat the cup down. "What?" Dr. Cheltenham continued staring at him without repeating the question. "No. Why?" "Well, I do." Dr. Jacobs continues to stare at Dr. Cheltenham with his mouth slightly open. "Harold, I have a cancer. My life expectancy is probably less than two months." Dr. Jacob's jaw drops even farther. "Hans, I'm so sorry. Of course, I want to be here for you. What can I do to help?" "Probably a lot more than you can imagine. What would you say if I told you that I had developed a method by which I can be put myself into a state of suspended animation that could keep me preserved, in my present state, for months and even years at a time?" "I'd say, you've been drinking too much of your wine," Dr. Jacobs commented without so much as a smile. Dr. Cheltenham rises from his chair. "Follow me, doctor."

The two head for the stairway leading to the basement. Dr. Cheltenham flips on the light switch and as they depart the bottom of the stairway, Dr. Jacobs looks around the basement. Not very impressive he thought. A desk, facing toward the center of the room, sat near one corner with a desk lamp on it and some papers laying on top. A swivel desk chair sat behind and a strait chair sat beside the desk. A bookcase lined the wall just to the side of the desk.

Dr. Cheltenham just stood by allowing Dr. Jacobs to take in all the simplicity of the room. Finally, Dr. Jacobs looks at Dr. Cheltenham quizzically. Cheltenham smiles and walks over to the bookcase. He removes five books from various shelves. As the last book came off the shelf the bookcase swings outward revealing a double door size opening and a stairway leading down into the dark.

Dr. Jacobs jaw dropped. "Come Herold. Welcome to my laboratory." Cheltenham starts down the stairs, flipping on a light switch just inside the door. The two made their way down into a yet lower room that was obviously underground located in the side yard of the house. A quick look around revealed a computer standing to his left. Beside the computer was a mag tape drive followed by four small cabinets and then what appeared as a printer. In front of the computer was a small desk with a CRT terminal and keyboard sitting. To his right was what appeared to be a metal tank about four feet wide and about seven feet long. Behind the tank was another enclosed upright tank resembling an oversized hot water heater. Plumbing appeared to connect the two tanks. In front and to the left was a cage with a chimpanzee inside. The most ominous was an opening in the far wall that appeared to be a natural tunnel leading off into the darkness.

Dr. Cheltenham was quiet while Dr. Jacobs tried to take everything in. Finally Cheltenham broke the silence. "I had this room built underground in my side yard. I told the workers it was a bomb shelter. It was the first thing I did to earn the local reputation of being eccentric. You notice the cave opening, over there. Several years ago, I was looking around to purchase property in this area. I followed the creek, outside, to a pretty little waterfalls. Further investigation revealed that a cave entrance, hidden by the falling water, existed just behind. I slipped thru the water falls and began following the cave. I estimate it continued for about two miles until it surfaced as a small opening in a ledge in the side yard of this house. At that moment I knew I needed to own this house. I wanted a secluded and secret place to continue my work."

Dr, Jacob stood silently listening. Dr. Cheltenham hesitated for Dr. Jacob to comment. With no sound coming forth, Cheltenham continues. This computer is the latest offering from NCR Computer

Company. It's an early prototype for communicating via a terminal with a TV screen and keyboard. No more punch paper cards. The operating system is called IMOS. These four smaller cabinets are hard drive storage units. Combined they hold one million bits of data. I call this system, my 'ID bank'." "ID Bank, like in Freud's ID?" Dr, Jacobs questioned. "Yes, well, more or less."

Dr. Cheltenham pauses, searching to find a starting place in what to tell Dr. Jacobs next. Slowly he begins. "Harold" [pause, then slowly and deliberately] "For years, now, I've been trying to find a way to use a healthy, but lifeless whole body as one single combination of organs that can serve as a donner body to someone else whose body has given out." "You mean like donating a heart to be transplanted into someone else with a bad heart?" Dr. Jacob asks. "Yes." "That's impossible," Jacobs said looking squarely at Dr. Cheltenham as if to determine his rationality. Cheltenham just smiled. "You should know me by know doctor. Impossible is not a word in my vocabulary. But, it does trigger my creative juices. In a nut shell, doctor, I have developed software and hardware that allows me to copy or move the images and the entire functions and memories of a person's brain and store it over there in my ID Bank." Dr. Jacobs glances at the computer assembly. Cheltenham continues, "Furthermore, I can restore the images into any lifeless human being, provided the body has been preserved very quickly after it's death. Over there, that tank, can preserve a person's body indefinitely.

Dr. Jacobs stood with his mouth hanging open once again. "So, this is what you propose to do to yourself?" "Yes, with your help. We'll move my brain to the ID Bank and then preserve my body in that tank until a cure for cancer can be found." "Hans, that could take years." I know. But I should be safe hidden here until that happens. Once you know of a cure for my cancer, all you need do is to come here and restore power to my lab and the computer will do the rest. After I'm back I'll accompany you to the place of cure."

Dr. Jacob's was totally speechless. When he was finally able to speak, "I don't . . . I don't know about all of this." "It's Ok," Cheltenham answered. "It is a lot to take in. Just work with me a couple days before you make any decisions. In the meantime, I have a little demonstration prepared for you."

Dr. Cheltenham walks to the Chimp's cage. He retrieves a banana from a small cabinet. Maggie eyes the treat as Dr. Cheltenham places it into a food dispenser attached to the Chimp's cage. "Watch this," Dr. Cheltenham says. Inside the cage were five small levers. As soon as the food hit the food dispenser, the chimp moved to the levers and pressed lever two and then lever four. A small door opens allowing the chimp to retrieve the banana. After the banana is consumed, Cheltenham produced another banana. "Maggie, this time press the levers wrong," he said to the chimp. He drops the banana into the food dispense. The chimp pressed lever five. Dr. Cheltenham turns toward Dr Jacobs. "Now the system is locked. It will not allow food to be retrieved unless he presses all levers starting with lever one. Maggie continues to look at Dr. Cheltenham for further instructions. "Ok, Maggie" The chimp immediately presses levers one thru five one at a time. After, she presses levers two and four and the food door opens.

After the second banana is consumed Dr. Cheltenham opens the cage door, the chimp immediately departs the cage into Dr. Cheltenham's arms. "Maggie, meet Dr. Jacobs." The chimp holds out her hand. Dr. Jacobs shakes her hand without a word. Dr. Cheltenham placed the chimp onto an examining table that stood next to the horizontal tank. He placed a metal cap onto the chimp's head and secured it with a strap under the chin. He also attached several monitoring tape patches to a few places on the chimp's body that he had previously shaved hair from. The chimp cooperated fully. Obviously, this was a familiar procedure for the monkey.

Dr. Cheltenham walks over the NCR 8264 computer terminal and types in a command. A few lights begin to blink on the computer's front side. The chimp, almost immediately, fell limp. Dr. Cheltenham walks over to Maggie. He looks up at Dr. Jacobs. "Come here and examine her." The doctor moves cautiously toward Dr. Cheltenham. Cheltenham holds out a stethoscope. "Here, Herold. Tell me if you are sure that this monkey is dead." Dr. Jacob took the stethoscope and leaned over Maggie. He could hear no heartbeat. That was no surprise, because he had already noticed the flatline on the heart monitor hanging beside the monkey. "Yes, you've managed to kill her. Very impressive," the doctor said sarcastically.

Dr. Cheltenham opened the plastic lid on the horizontal tank. Picking up Maggie, he placed her in the tank and closed the lid. Moving to the computer terminal he entered a command and the tank with Maggie inside filled with a pinkish liquid until the monkey was totally submerged in the tank. About an inch of liquid covered the outside of the plastic cover, therefore insuring absolutely no air inside the tank.

"Come, doctor, let's get some lunch. We'll return here tomorrow. I'm sure you have many questions.

After breakfast, the following day, Dr. Cheltenham and Dr. Jacobs descend to the laboratory for the beginning lessons on the procedure. Upon entering the lab, Dr. Cheltenham moves to the computer terminal. "I'm going to initiate the procedure to bring Maggie back to life. When you do this for me, all you will need do is restore electricity to the laboratory and the computer will do the rest."

Dr. Cheltenham types in a command and the hard drive storage devices whirl into life. Dr. Jacobs observes that the liquid in the tank is being drawn out. Maggie is laying on the bottom of the empty tank when suddenly her eyes opens and she begins to move around. Dr. Jacobs stares in amazement. "I'll be damned. The monkey is alive."

Dr. Cheltenham opens the tank lid and Maggie climbs into his arms. He walks her over the the examination table and removes the wire probes. Using a towel, he dries her from the wet liquid. He places her back into her cage and produces another banana. Dropping the banana into the food dispenser he commands Maggie. "Do it wrong, Maggie." The chimp presses lever number five then looks at Dr. Cheltenham for further instructions. "Ok, Maggie, fix it." The chimp presses all the levers from one to five then levers two and four. The dispenser door opened and the chimp retrieves the banana.

"I wanted you to see that Maggie is fully restored. From her point of view, all she remembers is that she was placed into the tank and one second later she was all wet." Dr. Jacobs nods in understanding but remains silent.

"I think, tomorrow we can put me into the tank and initiate the procedure." "So soon?" Dr. Jacobs exclaims loudly. "Yes. I'm feeling worse every day. The pains are getting unbearable." "But I haven't learned the system yet." "Actually, Doctor, you've learned all you need. Tomorrow all you need do is help hook up the electrodes to me and get me into the tank. After, you only need to go to the computer terminal and push the enter key. When the tank is full you can leave the lab. Take Maggie with you. Deliver her in Indianapolis to the address on the cage. They are expecting her. Close the bookcase door and pull the handle on the secret fuse box, out there in the basement. I'll show it to you in a minute. Grab your bags and go back home. This afternoon, I'll show you the cave entrance under the waterfalls. You may need to enter the lab from there if this house is occupied by someone when you return."

Dr. Jacobs stands almost in shock. Dr. Cheltenham looks at him for a few quiet seconds. "Will you help me, Harold?" Dr. Jacobs continues to stare at his friend. After what seemed like an eternity. "Hans, I will. I can't believe I'm saying that. I can hardly believe all I've seen here. I have to help you, not only because you are my friend but also to help you bring this amazing discovery to the world." "After you leave you must be prepared for the fact that I most likely will be suspended here for several years." Dr. Jacobs nodded he understood.

The following morning, Dr. Jacobs is standing beside his friend now all wired up and laying inside the horizontal tank. Having said their goodbyes, Dr. Jacobs walks over to the computer terminal. He turns for one last look at Dr. Cheltenham. Cheltenham smiles and nods for Jacobs to continue. Dr. Jacob feels as though he is about to push the execution button to an electric chair. He smiled at his old friend, turns and taps the enter key on the computer terminal keyboard. He watches as the light goes out of Dr. Cheltenham's eyes. Liquid begins to fill the tank. He continues to watch until the tank is full and the computer seems to go to sleep.

Dr. Jacobs can witness no more. He grabs Maggie's cage and climbs the stairs to the basement. Picking up the flashlight from the desk he carries a stool to the basement wall. Stepping onto the stool he reaches up and over the ledge to the hidden fuse box. Finding the lever, he pulls it to the off position. The entire basement goes dark. Using the flashlight, Dr. Jacobs climbs the stairs from the basement. His bags were already waiting by the front door. As he drives down the winding lane, he can hardly believe what he has just done. "I've just killed my best friend."

Chapter Four

Lonnie Meets Dr. Cheltenham

His eyes open as he lay, wet, in the bottom of the horizontal tank. Thoughts race through Dr. Cheltenham's newly restored mind. "Where am I. Oh, I remember. Dr. Jacobs must have brought me back. Maybe they have found a cure for cancer."

Dr. Cheltenham raises his head and looks around. The laboratory is empty. He slowly rises from the bottom of his tank. His muscles are stiff. He feels the familiar pane of his cancer. Removing the electrodes from his body, he climbs from the tank. "I wonder how long I've been in the preservation tank." Walking over to the computer terminal he glances at the date. His jaw drops as he reads May 19, 2020. "Oh, my God. It's been forty years." He stares at the terminal screen trying to clarify reality. "Where is Dr. Jacobs?"

Cheltenham walks to the entrance of the cave. He shouts into the darkness. "Harold!" No answer except his own echo. He moves to the steps leading to the basement. At the back of the secret bookcase door, he pears through the peep hole. The lights are off in the basement. "Someone must have found the secret fuse box and flipped it on. After all these years it is reasonable to assume someone has bought my house and is living here. If that's true they no doubt searched for why the basement lights didn't come on. That was short sighted of me. I should have kept them on the house circuit."

Dr. Cheltenham sat down in a chair to think. "For all I know, Herold may be dead. From how I feel I'm going to follow soon. I think the cancer has accelerated." He continued in thought, "I must find out if someone is living here." He rises and climbs the steps to the basement. Looking through the peep hole he notices that the lights are now on in the basement. "Well, someone is here." Then, at the edge of his lens he can see a man seated at his old desk.

The doctor turns and descends back to the lab. Sitting down he ponders his options. A plan emerges.

"I know I don't have long to live. I must act swiftly." After the doctor dresses himself, he picks up a syringe and fills it with a quick acting sedative. He hesitates for a moment. "I wish I didn't have to do this."

Climbing the stairs to the basement's secret bookcase door, he presses the unlock button and slowly pushes the bookcase open.

As Lonnie studies some of Dr. Cheltenham's notes at the basement desk, he is startled at the sound of the bookcase opening. Looking up, he sees the bookcase swinging open toward him. He is frozen with surprise and fear.

Dr. Cheltenham moves into view. "Hello. I didn't mean to startle you." Lonnie is still speechless. Cheltenham smiles. "I can tell from the look on your face that you didn't know about my secret entrance to the laboratory." The doctor takes a step toward Lonnie. Lonnie is still speechless but moves his head side to side. "I see you are reading some of my notes." He takes another step toward Lonnie. "I'm Dr. Cheltenham." Cheltenham takes one last step toward Lonnie and outstretches his hand.

Lonnie stands and takes the doctor's extended right hand. Quickly, Dr. Cheltenham pulls Lonnie forward over top of the desk. Before Lonnie can react, Cheeltenham stabs him in the buttocks with the syringe. Lonnie recovers quickly and pushes the doctor back. Dr. Cheltenham falls hard to the floor. "What did you do to me?" Lonnie asks loudly. The doctor doesn't answer. Lonnie leans over him and pulls him up into a sitting position. "I said, whaaaaat diii." Lonnie slumps onto Cheltenham's lap.

Looking toward the stairs leading up out of the basement, he hopes no one heard Lonnie. Quickly he struggles out from under Lonnie and begins to drag him toward the lab's stairway. Lonnie is heavy. It is all the doctor can do to move him. Once he and Lonnie are at the bottom of the stairs, he returns to the basement and shuts off the lights with the regular light switch. Returning to the lab entrance he closes the bookcase door.

He drags Lonnie toward the examination table and attempts to lift him. The doctor is just too weak. He decides to leave Lonnie laying on the floor. Removing Lonnie's shirt, he attaches the electrodes to his body. He then moves to the computer terminal and begins typing a new script file. Adding a 3-minute pause at the beginning of the script file, he executes the script.

Quickly he removes all his clothing. So much physical exertion has made it difficult to climb back into the horizontal tank. He attaches the electrodes and then lays back onto the bottom of the tank.

The computer comes to life. Dr. Cheltenham can hear the hard drives begin to hum. "It's only a matter of seconds now," he thought. His eyes close as his brain functions are moved into the ID bank. Immediately after, the computer moves Lonnie's brain functions into the ID bank as well. The final step is when it copies Dr. Cheltenham's brain functions into Lonnie's body.

Dr. Cheltenham grasps for breath. It was only a few seconds that Lonnie's body had stopped breathing before Dr. Cheltenham took over the task.

"I feel so strange. Something, I can't quite identify," the doctor thought. "I must act quickly to preserve my old body." He stands and removes the electrodes from Lonnie's body that he now possesses. Buttoning up his shirt he moves to the computer and enters a command. Immediately the horizontal tank begins to fill with the pink preservative liquid.

Giving thought to his next move he reaches into the back pockets of his trousers. He retrieves Lonnie's wallet to search for information. "My name is Lonnie Harris. I live in Queens, New York. I have some credit cards. Reaching into the front pocket of his trousers he finds an automobile key. He reads the tag on the key. "Avis Rent-a-Car, 2020 Toyota, red."

Dr. Cheltenham goes to the computer terminal and shuts down the computer system. He climbs the steps to the basement. Looking through the peep hole and finding the coast clear, he opens the bookcase door and steps into the basement. After closing the bookcase door and locking it, he removes three books that are unrelated to the key books that opens the bookcase thereby rendering the door unlockable. Gathering all his notes and manuscripts and the three books he heads up the basement steps, turns out the basements light and steps out into the entranceway of his house. Seeing no one, he moves to the front of the stairs leading to the bedrooms on the second floor. As he rounds the corner to the stairs, he sees Mike and Pam sitting in the living room. Fortunately, they are facing away from him. He quietly moves up to the bedrooms. Looking into both bedrooms, he sees Lonnie's open suitcase. "This must be my hosts room." He moves inside and quickly packs all of Lonnie's clothes into the two suitcases. He finds room for his manuscripts and the three books from the basement bookcase.

"Now, for the hard part," he thought. He moves down the stairs to the living room door. "Hi, friends." He speaks. Mike and Pam look up. "Hey guys. I'm sorry but I have received an urgent message from home. I must leave immediately." Both Pam and Mike rise from their chairs. "What is it Lonnie?" Pam asks with concern. "I'm sorry. I must go. I'll call you latter." Dr. Cheltenham turns quickly and darts out the front door. Pam and Mike look at each other and then rush to the front door. Cheltenham spies a red car. Pulling the car keys from his pocket, he entered the automobile, starts the engine and roars off down the lane.

After driving about two miles along the Indiana country road he pulls over and stops. He opens the glovebox. Inside he finds the rental papers from Avis. He also finds the return tickets on American Airlines to LaGuardia Airport in New York. He replaces the papers into the glovebox. Grabbing Lonnie's suitcases he departs the car and locks the doors. Looking up and down the road he moves into the woods. Arriving at the foot of the waterfalls, he darts under the falling water and into the entrance of the cave. Flipping on the lights, he starts through the cave tunnel toward his laboratory. Upon entering the laboratory he removing most of Lonnie's clothes from the suitcases. He then fills them with more of his notes and manuscripts. Switching off the light in the lab, he travels back through the caves entrance. Switching off the cave lights he again darts through the falling water. Back at the red Toyota he heads for the Indianapolis International Airport. His plan is to return the automobile and see if he can get an earlier flight to New York.

Chapter FIVE

Lonnie Harris/Dr. Cheltenham

The taxicab stops in front of the address printed on Lonnie's driver's license. Dr. Cheltenham pays the driver with money he found in Lonnie's trousers. Retrieving his suitcases, he walks toward the entrance to the apartment building. He has no idea if Lonnie lives alone or if he will find a wife or significant other, or even a roommate once he enters Lonnie's apartment. "I will just have to deal with whatever I find," he thinks.

Dr. Cheltenham reaches into his pants pocket for the keys he found there earlier. There are four keys on the ring. Trying each key, try number two turned the lock. Opening the door quietly, he enters the apartment. All is quiet. "Hello," he shouts. Listening, he shouts again. "I'm home." No answer. Cheltenham breathes easier. Sitting down his suitcases, he begins to explore the apartment. There are two bedrooms. One has obviously been turned into a home office. Upon examining the closet in the other bedroom, Dr. Cheltenham finds nothing except Lonnie's clothes. With a greater sigh of relief, Dr. Cheltenham realizes he has gotten lucky. Lonnie Harris appears to live alone.

Leaving his suitcases in the office bedroom, He sits down in a chair in the living room. This is the first chance he has had to relax since he came alive back in his laboratory. Sitting there, he ponders his situation. There was also the feeling that something was wrong. He first felt it almost as soon as he took over Lonnie's body. Thinking to himself, "I feel stronger than I have for years. It also feels good to be free of the cancer pain. So, what is this feeling of not belonging. Somehow, I don't feel alone in the body." "Get over it, Hans. Right now, I need rest. Tomorrow I must organize a plan," he said out loud.

The following morning, Dr. Cheltenham rises from bed at around 7:30. Eyeing the shower in the bathroom, he turns on the water and prepares to shower. Removing all his clothing, he admires his new, young body in the bathroom mirror. Suddenly, he feels as if he is invading someone's privacy.

After showering and a good shave. He goes to Lonnie's bedroom office and begins looking through the desk drawers and papers. After a time, he concludes that Lonnie must be a literary agent working for a company in New York City, The Robert Fryman Agency. "I should call them and secure a leave of absence," Cheltenham thinks. Looking around for a telephone book. "What kind of office or home doesn't have a telephone book," he says out of frustration. On Lonnie's desk, he sees a holder with business cards in it. They have Lonnie's name and phone number with the number of the Fryman Agency.

Lookng at the phone on the desk, Dr. Cheltenham sees that it doen'nt have a rotary dial, just a number pad. Punching in the Agency number he hears the familiar ring tones. "Robert Fryman and associates," the phone speaks into Cheltenham's ear. "Yes. Hi, this . . ." Cheltenham is cut off mid-sentence. "If you know your parties' extension, please enter it now. For accounting press 1. For sales press 2. If you are a publishing house press 3. For all other calls press 4 or stay on the line." Cheltenham presses 4. The phone rings in his ear. "Hello. This is Mildred. How can I make your day today." Dr. Cheltenham is almost speechless at such a greeting. Quickly composing himself, "Hi, Mildred. This is Lonnie Harris." He pauses hoping for a response. "Oh, hello Lonnie. How was your trip?" "Very good, thank you. Hey, I need to talk to the man." "The man?" she asks with surprise at Lonnie's reference to his boss. "Yes, you know. The head honcho, the big cheese." "I'll tell him what you called him." "Ha ha. Please don't." The phone rings. "This is Robert," was the businesslike voice coming back at Cheltenham. "Hi Robert. This is Lonnie." "Oh, hello Lonnie. Did you bring me back a manuscript from Michael?" "Ah." Cheltenham thinks quickly. So that's why Lonnie was in my house. There must be an author living there. "Well, no. But, he's working on it. It is almost done. We'll have it any day now." "Good. I'm tired of him dragging his feet. So, what's up? What's on your mind?" "Ah. Robert, something has come up. Something personal. I need to ask for a leave of absence." "What?" Robert nearly shouted into the phone. "What do you mean? For how long?" "At least two months."

"Two months. You can't do that to me." "I'm so sorry, but I have no choice. You'll probably need to assign another agent to my accounts." "What accounts. You only have Michael Martin." Dr. Cheltenham realizes he had made a mistake. "Well, you know what I mean. Of course, I mean Michael and any other accounts to be assigned to me in the future." Cheltenham crosses his fingers, hoping he has pulled the conversation out of the fire. "What is Michael going to say?" Robert asks. "I've already told him I have a family emergency. He'll be ok." So, what is this family emergency." "I'm sorry Robert. It's very personal. I'll fill you in when I get back. That is if you plan on having me back." "Oh, so that's how it is. Leave of absence or you are going to quit." "I'm sorry Robert." "Ok, you've got your leave." "Thanks. I'll be in touch," Cheltenham says as he hangs up the phone. He leans back with a great sigh of relief. "So far, so good ole boy," he says out loud, as though he was also talking to Lonnie. Suddenly his statement seemed strange even to him. "Now I need to find Harold."

The next morning Dr. Cheltenham picks up the receiver of the telephone on Lonnie's desk. He dials '0'. A voice comes back. "AT&T Assistance. Please state your request." "Yes, My name is Lonnie Harris and I am looking for the num . . " Lonnie Harris. What city please." "Ah, Philadelphia. His Name Dr. Ja . . . "One moment please. There is no listing in Philadelphia for a Lonnie Harris." "No, I'm Lonnie Harris. I'm . . . "AT&T Assistance. Please state your request." Cheltenham finally realizes that he is not talking to a real person. Hanging up the phone he leans back in the desk chair.

Looking around at the papers on Lonnie's desk he sees a pile of bills. The return address on one of the bills was Ace Parking Garage. He opens the envelop. It is an invoice for monthly parking.

"He must have a car. It could be in the parking garage, if he didn't drive it to the airport when he left for Indiana," he thought. Looking closer at the invoice it read, "2019 blue Lexus. Space B212." Cheltenham reaches into his pocket for the ring of keys. Inspecting each key, he found nothing that looked like an automobile key. He looked around the desk then opens the center door. There was a black, leather cased, item about two inches by 3 inches. It had buttons. Two of them were labeled with what looked like pad locks; one open, one closed. A third button showed the picture of a car with the trunk open and the word 'hold'. The last button was red with what looked like a horn blowing and the word 'hold.' The back side had a Lexus emblem. "Could this be a car key of some kind?" he thought.

The doctor packs a suitcase and with the Lexus leather case, he sets out to find Ace Parking. He thought better of asking someone where the parking garage was for fear he may be talking to someone who knows Lonnie Harris. Rounding the corner at the end of the block he spies the sign, "Ace Parking." Entering the parking garage, he sees an elevator. He enters the elevator and looks at the button panel. Buttons labeled with alphabetic letters instead of numbers. He presses 'B'. Stepping out of the elevator on level 'B' he begins looking for a blue Lexus and a space labeled B212. Just then he remembered the button on the leather case labeled as a horn. He pulled the case from his pocket and presses the horn button. Immediately he heard a horn honking in short beeps. The sound was coming from around the corner from where he was standing. As he rounded the corner the beeping stopped. He noticed parking numbers painted at the front of each space. Passing space 208 he looks ahead and sees a blue Lexus.

Standing next to the driver's door, he looks at the leather case, then at the driver's door. He decides to try the door to see if it is actually locked. The second he touched the door handle he heard a click and the door opened. "That's the dumbest thing I've ever seen," Cheltenham says to himself. "What's the point of locking a car if anyone can just open the door?"

He climbs into the driver's seat. Looking all around, he cannot see anyplace to insert a key. Then he sees a button that says start. Pressing the button, the instrument panel lights up. What looks like a TV screen in the center of the panel states, "PRESS BRAKE PEDAL BEFORE STARTING." Cheltenham stares at the message, then pushes down the brake pedal. He presses the start button and the Lexus roars to life. "That's even dumber than the door locks. Anybody could press the brake pedal and start the car and drive off." Shrugging, he puts the shifter level into DRIVE and departs the garage.

After about a three-hour drive, Dr. Cheltenham pulls up in front of the house where Dr. Jacobs lives. Or, at least where he lived forty years ago. It still looked the same as the last time he was there. Pressing the doorbell, Cheltenham had no idea who would answer. He wondered if he would recognize his old friend after 40 years. One thing for sure, the good doctor certainly will not recognize him.

The door opens. "Yes?" Cheltenham stares at the old man looking back at him. It was definitely Dr. Jacobs, but he couldn't believe how old the doctor looked. "What is it you want?" Dr. Jacob repeated impatiently.

"Hans . . ." "Do I know you?" Dr. Jacobs questioned. Dr. Cheltenham took a deep breath. He knew he needed to get Doctor Jacobs attention quickly before the door slammed shut on him. "Hans, forty years ago you visited Dr. Cheltenham in Indiana. He showed you something that was hard to believe. He asked your help to put him into a preserved state until a cure for cancer could be found." Dr. Jacob stood listening with his jaw dropped open. Dr. Cheltenham continued, "When Dr. Cheltenham first told you what he proposed you said you thought he had been drinking too much of his own wine." Cheltenham stops talking and waits for a response.

"Who are you? How do you know this?" "Harold, I am Dr. Cheltenham." He pauses again but Dr. Jacobs doesn't respond. "Herold, I know this is hard to comprehend. I think the owners of my old house must have found the secret fuse box and restored the power to the lab. When I came alive, I was in really bad shape. The cancer had progressed." Cheltenham pauses for a deep breath. "Herold, I borrowed this body from someone that was visiting." "Borrowed? Did you kill that person?" "No, he is stored in the ID bank. But I need your help to get him back into this body."

Dr. Jacobs shakes his head in disbelief. "Ok, come in." They enter the living room. "Have a seat, ah, Hans," he says obviously having trouble addressing his friend by name. "What do you have in mind. We still can't cure cancer." "I figured that," Cheltenham responds. "I have been doing a lot of thinking lately," Dr Jacobs continues. "You put a heavy burden on my life forty years ago. Lately I have realized that cancer will probably not be curable in my lifetime. I have had many sleepless nights thinking of you laying in that tank of liquid. Wondering if you were still there, wondering if I should check on you."

"I know Harold. I never expected so many years to go by. You have been a very good friend." Dr. Jacobs is silent. Dr. Cheltenham continues, "Harold, I still believe this process of mine needs to be perfected and presented to the world of science and medicine. I want to help make that happen. First of all, I need a human body to transfer into so I can give back this one to its owner." "You want a medical cadaver?" "No, I need a healthy body that has recently passed away within the last hour." "Whow! Where will you find that?" "I don't know. That is why I need your help." 'I guess you do."

"I've always kept in mind your discoveries and inventions. Especially after so many years has gone by. I've never revealed that anyone has actually perfected the process of mind transfer. There are only about three of my colleagues that has even consider the theory. Dr. Jacobs pauses in thought, looking down at the floor. Dr. Cheltenham remains quiet. Dr. Jacobs looks up at his friend. "We will definitely need their help." "Do you think we can count on them?" Dr. Cheltenham asks. "I don't know, but we'll definitely need to show them a demonstration."

Dr. Cheltenham momentarily looks away as he considers Dr. Jacob's last statement. Looking back at Dr. Jacobs, "Harold, we need to go to Indiana and get all my computer files and the ID bank." Dr. Jacobs thinks for a second then nods in agreement. "I just don't know how get a storage device as big as we will need." Dr. Jacobs smiles. "That's not the problem." Holding up his cell phone, "this phone has more memory and storage capacity than that entire dinosaur system you have in your lab." Dr. Cheltenham stares at Jacobs in disbelief. "No, the real problem is how to plug a modern storage device into an old, antiquated computer and have them be able to talk to each other." "I don't follow." "That's Ok. I know a guy. It won't be cheap."

Chapter Six

Return To The House Of Cheltenham

Two weeks later Dr. Cheltenham and Dr. Jacobs are in the living room at Dr. Jacobs house. "What time are they planning to arrive?" Dr. Cheltenham asks. "They are due here anytime now. Dr. Cheltenham eyes the strange device laying on the coffee table in front of him. A small box about half the size of a shoe box with a cable protruding from it's rear. On the end of the cable was an oversized plug that seemed completely out of place.

"Are you sure this gadget is going to work?" Cheltenham asks. "Well, my guy says it will. He said we need to find where your other hard drives are plugged into the CPU. If there is a vacant plug we can plug this into it. If not, he said we would need to unplug one of the existing hard drives and plug this one into its' port. He said this device will look like one of your existing hard drives. He also said you might have to 're-gen' the computer to get it to recognize a new device. Do you know how to do that?" "Yes, actually I do. Remember, I had to learn how to install that computer into my secret lab. I couldn't take a chance on anyone else knowing where the lab was."

The doorbell rings. "There's our guys," Dr. Jacobs says as he heads for the door. Dr. Cheltenham follows. As Jacobs opens the door Dr. Cheltenham sees a lady and two men. "Come in," Dr. Jacobs says as he greets his colleagues.

"I want you to meet my friend, Dr. Cheltenham. Hans, this is Janet Quinn and Herman Wiseman and Jerry Walker." They shake hands. "Come in and sit down." They all move to the living room and find seats. "So, what do we owe this invite into your home?" Janet asked. "We have some things to run by you guys. But first, how about a glass of wine all around?" Everyone nodded yes except Dr. Cheltenham. "I'll pass, thank you."

Dr. Jacobs passes out the glasses of wine and then takes his seat. Everyone takes a sip and then there is a moment of awkward silence. The trio sits their glasses down. They look back and forth between

Dr. Jacob and Dr. Cheltenham. Dr. Jacobs takes a deep breath and then begins.

"What I am about to say will be hard to believe but, please just hear us out. You know we have talked about the theory of mind transfer." Herman and Jerry trade glances and roll their eyes but remain quiet. Dr. Jacobs continues, "Dr. Cheltenham, here, is the one that introduced me to the idea, many years ago. He has done extensive research into mind transference." Everyone looks at Dr. Cheltenham. "Many years ago? What? When he was eighteen?" Janet asks.

Dr. Jacobs takes another deep breath, then continues. "In all of our talks I never actually mentioned that mind transference was not just a theory. Dr. Cheltenham has actually done it." Everyone looked quickly at Cheltenham. "Dr. Cheltenham did the first successful mind transference forty years ago." Herman shakes his head. "That's impossible. This guy couldn't possible be over forty years old. What's going on here Herold?"

"Dr. Cheltenham is my age, nearly eighty years old." There was a long pause before he continued. "Dr. Cheltenham came down with cancer over forty years ago. It was inoperable. That is why he accelerated his research. Forty years ago I helped him store his mind into a computer memory bank. Then he was immersed into a tank of liquid preservative, which I might add, he also perfected. He was to remain there until a cure for cancer was found. I was supposed to go back and revive him. We haven't found a cure for cancer yet. But, for some reason, his computer revived him. Realizing that his cancer was accelerating faster, he had to make a bold move."

Everyone looked again at Dr. Cheltenham. "Ladies and gentlemen, I borrowed this body from a man that happened to be visiting the house. I stored his mind into my computer and then transferred my own into his body." "I need your help to, first, return this body to its' owner, then, find a donner body for me. After that we can work together to perfect and introduce mind transference to the world."

"That's the craziest thing I've ever heard. This is some kind of joke," Jerry said. "I know it is hard to believe. We are prepared to prove it to you, but we need your help to do even that," Dr. Jacobs interrupted. The three guests looked at each other, then, Janet spoke, "What do you need from us?" "Dr. Cheltenham and I are going back to his secret laboratory in the heart of Indiana to copy all his computer files. This gadget laying here in front of you was specially designed to make it possible to get the files from such an old technology computer. While we are gone we need you to find us a facility where we can recreate his mind transference procedure in secret."

"Is that all?" Herman said sarcastically. "No, we also need a healthy body that has died and has donated himself to science for organ harvesting. We'll move the doctor into that body and restore this borrowed body back to its' owner.

"Ok," Janet speaks. Herman and Jerry stare at her in disbelief from this statement. "Look guys. We all know Harold. He's not crazy. If he says it, then its' true. Just think what mind transference would mean to the world." Jerry smiles, "Not to mention our reputations and bank accounts. I've always dreamed of a Nobel Prize." Herman looks at the two of them then down at the gadget on the coffee table. "So, a person's mind can fit into this little box?"

Dr. Cheltenham and Dr. Jacobs walk from the jet way at the Indianapolis International Airport on their way to baggage claim. "They said carousels six," Dr. Jacobs offers.

The two claim their luggage and head for the car rental counter. "Did you rent a jeep," Dr. Jacobs asks, remembering the lane leading up to the house. "No, we won't be going up the lane. I plan on us entering via the falls. No need to meet the occupants of the house."

Dr. Cheltenham parks at the side of the road. "We walk from here," Cheltenham says. They make their way through the woods and arrive at the foot of the falls. "If we pop thru quickly enough I don't think our bags will get too wet," Cheltenham offers. Once on the other side of the falls Dr. Cheltenham flips on the lights in the cave. Dr. Jacobs follows Dr. Cheltenham through the cave to the steps leading into the lab. Once inside the lab, Dr. Jacobs freezes at the sight of his old friend floating in the horizontal tank of preservative. Dr. Cheltenham notices his friend is frozen in a stare at the tank. "It must be weird for you, Harold." "It's mind boggling. It's surprisingly upsetting."

Dr. Cheltenham sits the storage gadget on a table and begins opening the back of the CPU. Dr. Jacobs turns his back on the tank. "So, what do you think?" he asks Cheltenham. Setting the back cover aside he pears at the ports that connect the hard drive units. "Well, unfortunately, there are no empty ports. I'll have to unplug one of the hard drives in order to plug in the device.

Dr. Cheltenham moves to the console and starts the computer booting up. "I will see if I can find enough room on three of the drives to hold what is on the fourth." How long will that take?" Jacobs asks. Not as long as it will take if we have to regen the system to get it to recognize the new device. That will take us well into the night." Dr. Cheltenham points to a box holding eight-inch floppy discs. "All those disks will have to be read in, questions answered and, with luck we won't get any read errors." What if we get a read error?" Jacobs continues to question. "Well, then we start over with the gen process." Dr. Jacobs quietly thinks, "Thank God for PC's."

With the computer purring and the hard drives humming, Dr. Cheltenham checks the directories of each hard drive along with the amount of free space. With a great sigh, "Ok, I have room to move everything form drive four to the other three drives. Shouldn't take more than an hour." Dr. Jacobs finds a chair and positions it so he can't see Cheltenham's body floating in the horizontal tank.

"Ok. Everything is moved onto the first three hard drives." Cheltenham executes the shutdown procedure to the computer. After all is quiet, he picks up the gadget and moves to the back of the computer. Unplugging hard drive number four, he plugs the gadget in. Returning to the computer console, he looks at Dr. Jacobs. "So far, so good. Frankly, I'm amazed that your hardware computer man was able to create a compatible plug on the end of his cable. It fit perfectly. I hope it's wired perfectly." "What if it isn't?" Cheltenham shakes his head and raises his eyebrows. "If it is wired wrong the computer won't see it and we'll think the computer needs to be genned. During the gen we will get errors but we will not know for sure that it is the gadgets fault. We'll have no choice but to do the gen several times before we finally give up." Dr. Cheltenham looks directly at Dr. Jacobs. "That could take days."

Dr. Cheltenham starts the computer re-booting. They both wait in silence. Finally, the computer console beeps and the word 'Ready' appears. "Well, at least it booted up." The doctor displays the directories of hard drives one thru three. "Looks good so far," he states, more to himself than to Harold. His hands are poised, motionless over the keyboard of the computer terminal. Finally he types, "DIR FOUR." Immediately the screen responds with the nearly empty directory of the gadget." "Oh, my God," Cheltenham gasps. "What?" Dr. Jacobs demands. Dr. Cheltenham turns in his chair. "It works. The computer thinks our gadget is hard drive number four. We are home-free. We don't need to re-gen the computer. When we get back to Philly I want to buy your computer friend the meal of his life."

Dr. Cheltenham turns back to the computer and initiates the moving of the files from his three hard drive to the gadget. Turning back to Dr, Jacobs, "We'll be out of here in no-time. Three to four hours at most."

Finally, back in Philadelphia, the two doctors are patiently waiting for their colleagues, Janet, Herman and Jerry, to arrive for their first meeting since Dr. Cheltenham and Dr. Jacobs return from Indiana. The doorbell rings and the five are seated in the living room.

"How was your trip?" Janet questions, initiating the start of the meeting. "It went better than we could have expected,": Dr. Cheltenham responds. "So, what's next? Herman asks, always coming right to the point. "Cheltenham responds, "We need a workplace to create our laboratory." "We've found an office space we think would work. It has 220-volt power and a private entrance to the parking lot. We should be able to come and go without notice," Janet answered. "They want a two-year lease with the first two month deposit," Herman added. "That should not be a problem. I'll cover it till we get some funding," Dr. Jacobs offered.

"The next challenge will be to find an NCR 8200 series computer," Dr. Cheltenham said. "What kind of computer is that?" Jerry inquires. "Nothing like any of you have probably seen. It's called a mini-mainframe computer straight out of the 80's." "Why can't we use a modern computer system?" Herman asks. "All my firmware and software and files are not compatible with today's technology." "I think that might be the perfect challenge for my friend who built the storage device," Dr. Jacobs suggests.

"So, what comes after that?" Janet asks. "We must find a body for me to possess. One that has been dead for less than two hours." "Oh, is that all? I'll run right out to Walmart and pick one up," Herman answered sarcastically. Janet frowns at him then offers, "First things first. Let's get a lab established."

One month later the five are standing in the middle of their new laboratory. The lab was fully equipped, including a working 8200 NCR mini mainframe. Dr. Cheltenham smiles as he looks around at what had been accomplished in so short of time. Then, he notices that everyone is looking at him with a smile that begged him to ask "What?"

The four looked at each other. Finely Janet spoke. "I think we have found a host body for you. The donner is brain dead on life support. The family plans to take him off life support in 3 days. His body is available for a medical school to use. Dr. Cheltenham asks quickly, "Can we get it?" "I think we can," Janet answered. "We put in a request using our new company name." "New company name?" Dr. Cheltenham asks. "Yes. Medical Research Labs, LLC," Janet continues. "So, you really think a new company has a chance?" Dr. Cheltenham presses. "Yes, because we offered $10,000 for it." Dr. Cheltenham's eyebrows raised. "That's a lot." "About twice the amount they could possible get anywhere else," Dr. Jacobs answered. Everyone is quiet as Dr. Cheltenham takes in all that has just been said. "Can we get the cadaver here in less than two hours?" Dr. Cheltenham finally spoke. "Yes. We stipulated immediate possession after flat lining. We used that as the excuse for offering so much money," Jerry explained, finally joining the conversation.

On the following Friday, at 10 a.m., a van pulls up to the labs private entrance. Herman and Jerry depart the van. Herman opens the back of the van door. Jerry reaches in and starts pulling out a gurney. Herman reaches for the other end of the gurney and as it clears the van the legs of the gurney drop down.

Dr. Cheltenham, along with Dr. Jacobs and Janet Quinn stand in the lab entrance waiting to receive the body. "Bring him in," Dr. Cheltenham orders. "Just push him over beside my computer terminal chair. You can leave him on the gurney." Herman and Jerry position the cadaver as directed. "Help me get the sheet off him. Then you can help me place the electrodes. After, you can help place electrodes on me in the same manner." "What do we do with the body you are in now?" Jerry asks. Dr. Cheltenham and Dr. Jacobs glace at each other. "I'll still be in this body. You understand the difference between a computer file being copies and one being moved. We are simply copying my current mind into this body." Herman gasps, "You are going to exist with yourself at the same time." "Yes. It is necessary until we get back to the Indiana lab so I can restore this guy to himself." "That is just too weird," Herman says shaking his head.

With both Dr. Cheltenham and the cadaver hooked up, Dr. Cheltenham asks everyone to be very quiet. "I've never did the transference this way before. I want my brain as inactive as possible during the transference." Dr, Cheltenham executes the mind transference program on the computer terminal. The four watch in awe. After four minutes Herman takes in a sudden breath. "That guy just blinked his eyes." Everyone looks at the cadaver. The body began to move, slowly at first. Breathing become more predominate. Finally, the cadaver attempted to speak. Everyone is speechless. "Please, don't refer to me as 'that guy'. My name is Dr. Hans Cheltenham."

The two Cheltenhams begin removing the electrodes from their bodies. "Please get me some clothing," the newly imprinted Dr. Cheltenham requested. "From now on please address only me. I want the other me to absorb as little as possible. Whatever the other me experiences from this second on, will be lost when he is restored with Lonnie's memory."

The two Dr. Cheltenham's and Dr. Jacobs pull off the side of the road in Indiana. Driving from Philadelphia was easier than finding ID for two Dr. Cheltenhams. Picking their way through the forest, they dive under the waterfalls and enter the cave leading to the secret lab. Upon entering the lab Dr. Cheltenham starts the boot-up process on the computer. He nods at Lonnie's body to lie down on the examining table. "I'm going to give him a sedative that will put him to sleep. He'll be out for a couple hours."

After hooking up the electrodes to Lonnie's body, Dr. Cheltenham moves to the computer terminal. "The first step is to erase my mind from his brain. After, I will restore his original mind. When he wakes up, he'll probably think he had just fallen asleep. We'll put him into my desk chair up in the basement. That is the last place he will remember being, before I kidnapped him. We'll have time to get out of here before he wakes up."

Chapter Seven

Lonnie Awakes

Lonnie slowly gains consciousness. He raises his head from the desktop. Looking around, he tries to make sense of the last thing he remembered. The basement looked the same to him. The lights were on. The papers he was reading were laying on the desk in front of him. "I must have been dreaming," Lonnie thinks to himself. "It seems so real." He looks at the bookcase that had opened up when Dr. Cheltenham appeared. Getting up from the desk, Lonnie goes to the bookcase and checks it out thoroughly. It did not seem to be anything but a simple bookcase mounted to the basement wall. "I got to quit reading his stuff. I think it is getting to me." Lonnie laughs at himself and heads for the basement stairs. Flipping off the light, he walks out into the entrance hall. He finds Mike and Pam sitting in the living room.

"Hi guys." Mike and Pam jerk their heads around. "Lonnie? When did you get here?" Mike questioned. Both Mike and Pam stare at Lonnie with their mouths open. "Heh? What do you mean? You know when I got here." "We didn't hear you drive up or come in," Pam said. Lonnie looks at the two with confusion written all over his face. "Ah. I've just been in the basement reading Cheltenham's notes. I think I fell asleep. How long was I down there anyway? What time is it?"

Mike and Pam are speechless. "What's the matter with you guys?" Lonnie asks. Mike finds his voice. "We are just so surprise to see you after all this time, especially since the way you left." "Left? Left where? When?" "Two months ago. You came up from the basement, grabbed your bags, jumped into your rental car and roared off down the lane."

"What are you talking about? I haven't left since I got here yesterday. If this is a joke, you got me." Pam and Mike look at each other. Neither one can think of what to say. Mike looks back at Lonnie. "Lonnie, you haven't been in this house for the last two months. We received word from our agency that you were taking a leave of absence. Something to do with a family emergency." Lonnie looks at them, then grins. "Come on guy. Enough is enough. You got me." "The agency has assigned another agent to us."

Lonnie's smile fades away. Everyone is silent. Lonnie realizes that this is not a joke. Pam and Mike are serious about what they are saying. His memory goes back to the dream he had in the basement. After a long stare at both Pam and Mike he asks, "What is the date today." "August fourteenth," Mike answers. Lonnie is silent. He walks over to a chair and sits down. "I don't know what is going on. All I remember is that I was sitting at the old desk on the basement. I think I fell asleep. I had a weird dream. After I woke up, I came up here." Lonnie pauses in thought. "This should be June 18. It was when I when down into the basement this morning." Lonnie stops again. In trying to make sense of it all he asks, "If I left two months ago, how did I get back into your basement?" Pam and Mike continue to look at Lonnie but did not answer. Lonnie jumps up and peers out the front living room window. "Where's my rental car?"

Lonnie looks back at Mike. "Don't say it. I know. I drove it off two months ago." Lonnie turns, walks to a chair in the living room and sits down. Mike and Pam do the same. Everyone is silent. Lonnie tries to make sense of the situation. He feels he is on the verge of a mental breakdown.

Pam rises from her chair. "I think I'll get us something to eat."

Lonnie and Mike continue to sit quietly. Finally, Lonnie looks up at Mike. I need to get back to New York. I don't know what is going on but I can't figure it out from here." "I'll try and get you a flight out." Mike offers. "Do you want to fly from Indy or Cincinnati?" "I don't care. The earliest flight possible. Cincinnati is closest."

Lonnie is in deep thought while sitting in the economy seat of United airlines headed for LaGuardia airport. Thinking to himself, "I don't know if I still have an apartment. Rent hasn't been paid for two months. I wonder if my car is still in the parking garage at my apartment. I'll go to the agency and see if I can get my old job back." Lonnie continues to ramble in his mind. "Who am I kidding. I can't just go back as though nothing has happened. I must get answers, and soon, or I will lose my mind.

The Uber driver pulls up in front of Lonnie's apartment. With a 'thank you' Lonnie departs the automobile. He heads for the parking garage. Entering the elevator, he punches the 'B' for the floor where he left his car. The elevator door opens and Lonnie departs. He walks to the left and around the corner to space 212. There is his blue Lexus. "I wonder if the battery is dead," Lonnie thinks to himself. Reaching into his front pant pocket he retrives the Lexus key. Punching the door lock button the Lexus doors instantly unlock. "Well, that's encouraging," he thought.

Sliding into the drivers seat and with his foot on the break Lonnie pushes the start button. The Lexus roars into life. Sitting there with the engine running, he looks around the car. Everything seemed normal but he had the feeling someone besides him had been in the car.

After departing the car he heads for his apartment. His key worked so he must not have been evicted. Entering the apartment Lonnie looks around. It only took a few seconds for Lonnie to realize someone else had been living there. Many things were out of place. Even his clothes were arrange differently in his closet.

Lonnie decides to go to the apartment building office. Upon entering the lady behind the desk looks up. "Hi Lonnie," she says. "Hi Maxine." "How can I help you?" she asks. "I was just wondering if I was caught up on the rent for this month." Maxine looks surprised. "Well, of course. You were just in here a few days ago and paid." "I was?" Lonnie continued. "Are you sure it was me or did I send someone?" "It certainly was you, but," Maxine's voice lowered without finishing the sentence. "But what?" Lonnie pressed. "Well, you seemed preoccupied. You were in a hurry. Usually you are in here teasing me. Don't you remember?" "Yes, of course. I remember now. Sorry, I've just got a lit on my mind right now. I'll see you next month." Lonnie departed, now more confused than ever. How could he have just lost 2 months of memories?

Lonnie returns to his apartment. Sitting behind his desk with his head buried in his hands he feels he is close to losing it. Maybe he should call his doctor. Perhaps the doctor could recommend a psychiatrist. Maybe under hypnosis he could recall the last two months. After pondering this idea for nearly two hours Lonnie reaches for his cell phone to call the doctor. Just as the screen on his phone comes alive there is a knock on the door. Lonnie rolls his eye and shakes his head. "It never fails."

Lonnie opens the door. Standing there is a handsome gentleman of about thirty-five years old. "Can I help you. I'm not buying anything if that is what you want." The gentleman smiles. "May I come in? I would like to explain to you why you have memory loss of the last two months." Lonnie nearly falls over. How can this man know about my memory loss.

"Please, can I come in and explain? My name is Dr. Hans Cheltenham. We met once but you thought it was a dream."

Lonnie stares at Dr. Cheltenham. Slowly Lonnie begins to speak. "In my dream, you were much older."

"Please let me come in. I want to explain and I think you need to hear," Cheltenham persisted. Lonnie turns aside and waves Dr. Cheltenham in. "You can sit on the couch." Lonnie takes the easy chair opposite.

'Lonnie, what I am going to tell you will be a little hard for you to hear. But, please wait until I finish for questions." Lonnie makes no jesters; only continues to stare at the Doctor. "Think back to when you were in the basement of the Indiana house. You think you fell asleep reading my manuscripts. You had a dream that someone came out of the bookcase. Lonnie, what you thought was a dream was not. I actually came out of the bookcase and I really did pull you over the desk and sedate you."

Lonnie's lips parted. He started to say something but the Doctor cut him off. "I know the man you saw come out of the bookcase did not look anything like me now."

Dr. Cheltenham relays the last two months to Lonnie in great detail. At the end Lonnie was not sure what to say or how to feel. He definitely felt violated. The Doctor had lost him his job. Who knew what else the Doctor had screwed up pretending to be him.

Finally Dr. Cheltenham breaks the silence. "Lonnie, you have every reason to hate me for what I have done to you. I sincerely ask for your forgiveness. I know I've lost you your job with the Fryman Agency. But, I promise that I have been careful in my pretense to be as disruptive as possible." Cheltenham reaches inside his suit pocket and retrieve an envelope. Handing it to Lonnie he says, "Here is a check for the rent of your body for two months. I hope it will tie you over until you get re-established with employment.

Lonnie opens the envelop and retrieves the check. His eye brows raise as he sees the $50,000 number printed on the check.

Dr. Cheltenham rises to depart. Lonnie looks up from the check. "Doctor, this mind transference procedure you hope to develop for all of mankind, have you considered the possibility that this sort of thing should not be done?" Cheltenham looks surprised. "What do you mean? Wouldn't anyone, even you, want to live for ever?"

Lonnie hesitates before speaking. "Doctor, do you believe in God?" Cheltenham is suddenly uncomfortable. "Well. Lonnie, I am a scientist. If I can't see it or feel it or prove it I pretty much have to disqualify it until it is proven. Does that answer you question?'

The Doctor heads for the door. "Just one more question, Doctor, please." Cheltenham stops and turns toward Lonnie. "Doctor, was my body ever totally dead?" Cheltenham hesitates just looking at Lonnie then slowly answers. "No, I moved your mind into my ID bank at the same time I copied my mind into you brain. Your body was never actually dead." "Tell me, doctor, while you occupied my body for these two months, how did you feel?" "I don't know what you mean?" "Were you as comfortable in my body as in your own?" Cheltenham looked down at the floor pondering as to whether he should answer truthfully. Finally looking up, "All the time I occupied your body I felt like I was an intruder. I felt I didn't belong." "Then answer me this. Was the body you now occupy ever totally dead." "Yes." "Do you feel that way in this body?" "Well, actually, no." "So how do you feel in this body?" Again, Cheltenham looks down before answering. The truth was that the good Doctor had been worrying about his strange sensation while occupying other bodies. "No. It is different with this body. I feel strangely alone, almost lost."

"Dr. Cheltenham, I thank you for the check. I certainly can use the money." Dr. Cheltenham open the door to depart. "Doctor. One more thing. You say you need proof that there is a God. I suggest the feelings you felt occupying a body that had never died and the feelings you feel occupying a body that has experienced death might be the beginning of that proof." Cheltenham didn't know how to respond to that statement. He simply nodded and smiled and walked away.

Chapter Eight

It Starts

Early Monday morning the five are seated around their make-shift conference table. "I want to thank Jerry for finding this facility. It is perfect for our needs at this time," Dr. Cheltenham begins. Dr. Jacobs seconds that. Herman chimes in. "I second that. All in favor say 'Aye'." They all laugh.

"OK, guys. So much for your first motion. Premature I might add," Pam says. "Now we need to focus on structure," Pam continues. "What do you think of 'Cheltenham Industries, Inc.' for the main corporate name?" The five look at each other. "So I guess Wiseman Industries is out," Herman spout sarcastically. The four stare at him. "OK, OK. Just kidding. Cheltenham Industries is fine."

Janet rolls her eyes and continues. "Since Drs. Cheltenham and Jacobs are funding this enterprise, I suggest we split the new corporation by giving twenty-six percent to each of them. We three can split the rest." Janet stares at Herman. "That's sixteen percent for each of us, Herman. But you can do the math later after you remove your shoe to count your toes. Herman smirks at her.

Dr. Jacobs jumps in. "That sounds fair to me. What do you think, Hans?" "Yes, that is fine." "Good, Janet continues. "So that is settled. I think we will want to create sub-siderites for the different divisions of marketing." "Such as?" Jerry questions. "Such as a division dedicated to receiving and storing billions of minds into Dr. Cheltenham's ID bank. I think we will have three divisions. I suggest that each one of the three of us be made responsible for one of the divisions. That person should be bonused with the continued success of his or her division. The Doctors will oversee the entire operation. "I think all of that is fine," Dr. Cheltenham says. "I leave all that legal stuff up to you guys. I want to concentrate on mind transference procedures." "Yes, I concur. But, Hans, you must keep in mind, we will need to be ready to handle millions of customers in a short time. If we are not ready, our success could also be our demise," Dr. Jacobs adds.

Dr. Cheltenham nods as he begins to consider the magnitude of what Harold has just said.

Ok, I'll get started on the legal stuff. Hans and Harold can begin organizing their lab. Jerry, Herman, you two begin exercising your creative juices. We are going to need some real marketing strategies," Pam added. The five depart.

Ten Years Later -- 2030

Cheltenham Industries has grown to be the biggest corporation on the planet. The new facility is in a perfectly round building with a diameter of one mile. The very center is a court yard covered with a clear acrylic dome. The round hallway has offices and laboratories on both sides. A single car horizontal elevator runs around the entire circle of offices. Hanging from the above track, it travels to any room depending on the number you enter. Each doorway has a call button.

Dr. Cheltenham is still occupying the same body however Dr. Jacobs has claimed one of the newly cloned models. As a handsome twenty-four year old man he is still trying to get comfortable with the feeling that he is so alone in the new body. "I just can help but feel that the most important part of me is missing," Dr. Jacobs says while seated across from Dr. Cheltenham's desk. "I know Harold. I don't think the feeling ever goes away. You should go to the psych department. They are dealing with this problem remotely for the millions that feel that way after receiving their new bodies. Speaking of new bodies. How do you like yours?" Dr. Jacobs smiles and says, I think I am quite handsome for an old man. I can't get over how limber this body is. I think I'll keep this one for a while."

"Herald, I want to run something by you," Dr. Cheltenham says slowly. Dr. Jacobs sits quietly waiting for Dr. Cheltenham to begin. After a long pause and careful thought of how to began, Dr. Cheltenham say, Harold, I have been thinking. Do you remember Lonnie Harris?"

"Yes. The guys body you stole in the beginning." "Borrowed, Herold, borrowed." Jacobs nods with a smile. "Something Lonnie said just before I left his house." "You went to his house?" "Yes, I felt I owed him an explanation. He was in agony wondering how he lost 2 months of his life. After I told him what we did I gave him a check for fifty thousand dollars." Dr. Jacobs looks surprised but only nods approval. "Just before I left his house he ask me if I believed in God. Of course, I said no. I told him I only believed in things I could prove or see. Then he asked me how I felt in this new body. When I told him I felt so alone as though some of me was missing, he said the strangest thing. He said those feeling I was having might be the proof of God I needed." "How strange. What could he have meant?" "That's what I want to talk to you about. I think Lonnie and all other Christians, along with every other religion in the world, are trying to make since of the concept of death. They all look forward to meeting a supreme being that will Concore death forever." Dr. Cheltenham pauses.

Dr. Jacob is patiently waiting for Dr. Cheltenham to continue. The silence goes on too long. "So what is you point?" Dr. Jacobs finely blurts out.

Dr. Cheltenham remains silent. He simply looks at Dr. Jacobs as he ponder what next to say and what he should keep to himself. Finely he speaks. "Harold, I think I am the god they are looking for. I have brought them endless life. My mind transference has been perfected to such a high level that anyone who chooses can now have their mind files, that we house here, updated each night as they sleep. Even if they meet with a catastrophe the following day, they will be restored with only a few hours of lost memory. Furthermore, your new clone bodies are very nearly reaching the ability to live for two hundred years. The only thing missing is someone to give them hope for the future. A future that will last for ever."

Dr. Jacobs sits quiet/ He is stunned at his friends conclusions. He parts his lips to speak then doesn't. "Harold, if I become their god I will be able to eliminate all manner of bad goings on here on earth. Just think about it. No more wars, no more famine or hungry people. Everyone can live in peace in a comfortable life style." Dr. Jacobs shakes his head, then speaks. "I don't know Hans."

Dr. Cheltenham suddenly dawns a serious look and then speaks with a strange sounding authority in his voice. "I do know Harold. I have spoken and it shall be. From this moment on, Harold, I am no longer to be addressed as doctor or Hans, but rather Father Cheltenham. So be it. So it is." Dr. Jacobs suddenly felt his blood turn cold.

Cheltenham Industries continues to flourish. Production of human clones has been perfected to the point where the human body has a life expectancy of around one-hundred and twenty-five years. Resistance to disease is high. In the ID department where minds are stored and updated on a daily basis, alterations are made to enhance a persons peaceful existence.

However, Cheltenham is concerned about the resistance coming from the Christian community. They still refuse to accept mind transference. All who choose to transfer their mind and have it updated daily are required to have a QR code permanently placed on their forehead. All newly created cloned bodies have a QR code imbedded on their hand. The Christian community are the only humans left without such marks.

For some time now, Dr. Cheltenham has been amassing an army to ensure peace through the world. Together with his army he is enforcing his law that no one is allowed to purchase goods or food unless they have one of the marks either on their forehead or on their hand. But the Christians have managed to survive with their own underground purchasing power.

"I have instructed my army to search out these Christians and offer them one last chance to join us. If they refuse I have order them to be put to death on the spot," Cheltenham announces to the heads of his company. All bow in approval. "Yes father." They all chant in unison. Only Dr. Jacobs is silent, only mouthing the words. Cheltenham continues, "We have made such great strides. Except for the Christians, the world now knows peace in a way never before achieved. Soon, the Christians will be gone, if not by my armies hands then by simply death by old age. Once we are rid of them I will truly be god to all." "All praise to father Cheltenham," they chant. Dr. Cheltenham eyes his old friend, Dr. Jacobs. "Harold, I want you to have the latest model of one of our newly cloned bodies. You will find more peace. Go immediately and pick one out and make the transference." Dr. Jacobs nods.

Forty Years Later – 2070

Dr. Cheltenham sits high on his throne in the middle of the enclosed courtyard at Cheltenham Industries. The entire world is now composed of cloned humans. All are required to make a pilgrimage at lease once per year to pay respect and pray to Dr. Cheltenham. However, this day he is troubled. He had a strange dream last night. He dreamed that Lonnie Harris appeared to him. "What you don't understand, Doctor, what you have never understood, is that you actually died in 1980 when Dr. Jacobs moved your mind into the ID bank and drowned you in a vat of preservative. What came back alive forty years later was only an image of you. You were not your body. You were not your mind. You were the spirit that lived inside you. A spirit put there by God. Yes, God. The very one you refuse to recognize. You are no longer here. You have not been here for ninety years. That empty feeling you have carried with you all these years is your mind missing the real you."

Cheltenham could still hear Lonnie from his dream. "Enough! Enough of this foolishness. I need to call a meeting with my principals."

Dr. Jacobs, Janet Quinn, Herman Wiseman and Jerry Walker hustle into the throne area as summoned. Cheltenham seemed agitated. "Harold. Why is it you always seem to be distant. I don't think you really worship me," Cheltenham yells at Dr. Jacobs. Don't you know yet that I AM GOD."

Dr. Jacobs stares at Cheltenham, but before he could speak, a loud voice fills the air. **"You are not God. You have created nothing."**

Everyone looks around. At first they could not see anything. Then, slowly, they became aware of what appeared to be a round spherical area that shimmered and blurred. The voice was coming from there. **"Cheltenham, you have destroyed everything beautiful that my Father and I created. All that is left here on earth is a world of zombies. Humans without their souls. Their spirits have long left this earth. You are nothing."**

"Who are you? How dare you speak to me this way." **"SILENCE screamed the blurry sphere. IT IS FINISH!**

The five are a speechless. They watch, helplessly, as the sphere began to grow. Soon, it filled half of Cheltenham's throne room. As it continued to grow the five began to back up until they were against the back wall of the court yard. The sphere ultimately consumes them. Then it consumes all of Cheltenham Industries' large complex. The sphere grows ever large until finally in has consumed all of the earth. Ever growing until it finally consumed all of the universe.

Finally, it faded away. Nothing left except a great VOID and a new Heaven and a new Earth.

The End